A JUST ONE MORE BOOK
Just For You

The Singing Dog

by Valerie Tripp

Illustrated by Sandra Cox Kalthoff

Developed by The Hampton-Brown Company, Inc.

CHILDRENS PRESS ®

CHICAGO

Word List

Give children books they can read by themselves, and they'll always ask for JUST ONE MORE. This book is written with 77 of the most basic words in our language, all repeated in an appealing rhythm and rhyme.

all	first	o'clock	today
along	for	of	town
am	four	old	tree
and	friend(s)	on	Turtle
are		one	
as	get	only	under
at	go(ing)		us
	Goose	play(ed)	
be		prize	wants
Bear	he		way
big(gest)	hello	ride(s)	we('ll)
but	his	Rufus	what
			when
can't	I('m)	see	who(m)
	in	show	will
do	is	sing(ing)	win
does	it	sings	won
dog		slow(ly)	
	just	song	yes
each			you
elephant	know	the	your
end(s)		there('s)	
	more	they	
	music	this	
	my	time	
		to	

Library of Congress Cataloging-in-Publication Data

Tripp, Valerie, 1951-
The singing dog.

(A Just one more book just for you)
Summary: On his way to the music show where he hopes to win the biggest prize, Rufus the singing dog meets many animal friends with the same idea in mind.
[1. Dogs—Fiction. 2. Animals—Fiction. 3. Stories in rhyme] I. Title. II. Series.
PZ8.3.T698Si 1986 [E] 86-14797
ISBN 0-516-01578-8

Copyright ©1986 by Regensteiner Publishing Enterprises, Inc. All rights reserved. Published simultaneously in Canada. Printed in the United States of America.
1 2 3 4 5 6 7 8 9 R 90 89 88 87 86

Here is Rufus,
singing his song,
singing his song
as he rides along.

The singing dog
is on his way
to the music show
in town today.

He rides and sings
and sings and rides.
He wants to win
the biggest prize.

He rides and sings,
and whom does he see?
His old friend Goose
is under the tree.

Hello, Goose!

Are you going my way?

Are you going to the show today?

Yes, I am!

I'm going your way.

I'm going to the show today.

The old friends sing,
and sing and ride.

Each wants to win
the biggest prize.

On they go,
and whom do they see?
It is Bear, as big as can be.

Hello, Bear!

Are you going my way?

Are you going to the show today?

Yes, I am!

I'm going your way.

I'm going to the show today.

The old friends sing,
and sing and ride.

Each wants to win
the biggest prize.

On they go,
and whom do they see?
It is Turtle,
going slow, s-l-o-w-l-y.

Hello, Turtle!
Are you going my way?
Are you going to the show today?

Yes, I am!
I'm going your way.
I'm going to the show today.

The old friends sing,
and sing and ride.
Each wants to win
the biggest prize.

On they go
to the music show.
And when they get there,
what do you know?

The elephant is in the way.

Show ends

at 4 o'clock

You CAN'T be in the show today.
This music show will end at four.
There's only time for
JUST ONE MORE!

Only one?
What will we do?"
One of us can go,
but WHO?"

The old friends know
just what to do.
Go on, you sing!
We'll play for you.

They played for Rufus,
and what do you know?
All four won first prize
at the music show!

E
T

Tripp, Valerie

The singing dog

DATE DUE

BRODART		04/88	9.67
APR 1 3 1989 9	APR 2 0 1989		
20			